EASY
NICKELS

EASY NICKELS

AND OTHER HUMOROUS STORIES
Compiled by the Editors
of
Highlights for Children

Compilation copyright © 1995 by Highlights for Children, Inc.
Contents copyright by Highlights for Children, Inc.
Published by Highlights for Children, Inc.
P.O. Box 18201
Columbus, Ohio 43218-0201
Printed in the United States of America

ISBN 0-87534-636-7

Highlights is a registered trademark of Highlights for Children, Inc.

CONTENTS

EASY NICKELS

By David Lubar

Timmy was reaching for a drinking straw in the back of the kitchen cabinet when he knocked over the pepper. The jar fell from the shelf and hit the counter. "Uh-oh," Timmy said, catching it as it bounced. The jar didn't break, but the top fell off and a cloud of pepper spilled out.

Just then, his little brother, Sam, walked into the kitchen, right into the middle of the pepper cloud. Sam stopped, his nose twitched, he took a quick, deep breath, and "Yaaatchhhooeee!" he sneezed a hard sneeze. Something bright flashed past Timmy's head and hit the refrigerator. It clinked off the door of the fridge, flew past his head again, then hit the floor.

"Gosh," Timmy said, looking down. There, spinning on edge, was something shiny. It spun for another moment, then clattered to a stop, lying faceup on the linoleum. Timmy stared for a while, amazed by what he saw. It was a nickel.

"Blettchhhoooo!"

Timmy ducked as another nickel shot past him, nearly hitting him in the ear. It bounced off the edge of the counter and landed in the sink with a clatter. "Hey, Sam, how'd you do that?"

"Don't know," Sam said, sniffling and wiping his nose.

"Can you do it again?"

"Don't know."

"Kate, get in here," Timmy called. His sister had to see this. "Come on, hurry up."

"What is it?" Kate asked, running into the kitchen.

"Sam can sneeze nickels. Show her, Sam. It's really neat." Timmy waited for his brother to do the trick again.

Kate gave Timmy an angry look. "Now that's just ridiculous."

"Come on, Sam," Timmy urged. "Do it again."

"I can't just sneeze," Sam said.

Timmy picked up the pepper. *Maybe I shouldn't,* he thought, but he had to find out. This was too wonderful to leave alone. He poured out a handful of pepper and tossed it in Sam's direction. The cloud floated toward his brother as if it were seeking a place to land. It surrounded his head.

Nothing happened for a moment. Sam blinked. Sam sniffed. "Kaaatchooo!!!!!" Sam shot another nickel across the kitchen.

"Wow!" Kate exclaimed.

Timmy imagined mountains of nickels filling the house. "We're rich!" he said.

"Gacheeeoooo!!!" Sam said, adding to the wealth.

In half an hour, the three kids had a pile of nickels and an empty pepper bottle. Sam, aside from looking a bit red in the eyes, didn't appear to be harmed in any way by this new ability. He seemed to be enjoying the attention he was getting from his older brother and sister.

"Now what?" Kate asked, holding up the empty bottle of pepper.

"I'll go to the corner and get some more. You count the money." Timmy got his jacket and went outside. Excited at this great new business, he ran to the store. He'd forgotten to take any of the nickels, but he still had some of his allowance left in his pocket. He bought a bottle of pepper and ran back home, already thinking about how he was going to spend his share of the wealth.

"Here's the pepper," he said, bursting into the kitchen. He put the bottle down and filled a glass of water from the sink. The run had made him a little thirsty.

"Great," Kate said. "We counted the nickels." She pointed to the neat stacks of coins on the kitchen table.

"How much?" Timmy asked.

"One dollar and forty-five cents," Sam said, smiling. "Kate says that's almost fifty cents for each of us."

Timmy's dreams crumbled. All he could say was, "Oh no."

"What is it?" Kate asked. "What's wrong?"

Timmy held up the bottle of pepper and pointed to the price tag. "This cost $1.52," he said. "And we made $1.45 from the nickels. Every time we do this, we'll lose seven cents."

"Too bad Sam can't sneeze quarters," Kate said.

Timmy looked at his brother, then at the pepper, then at the spice cabinet. "Maybe there's something that will make him do that. This was only black pepper. What if we tried something real hot like red pepper? Maybe we *could* get quarters."

"No, not quarters," Sam said, running from the room with his hands in front of his nose.

Timmy and Kate looked at each other, then shook their heads. As tempting as it was, they couldn't do that to Sam. "I guess we're out of business," Timmy said, though it was a shame not to give it one little try. He took a sip of water. It went down the wrong way. He started coughing. Something shot from his mouth. It clinked to the floor.

"Quarter?" Timmy asked when he finally got his breath back.

Kate shook her head. "Just a penny."

Timmy sighed. It was going to be a long day.

Animal, Vegetable, or Plastic?

By Harriett Diller

Bert slammed her books on the library table she was sharing with Dalton. "You know what makes me madder than a rattlesnake?"

"People who tie your shoelaces together?" asked Dalton, glancing up from his science book.

"Plastic plants!" Bert pointed to a tall plastic palm tree next to the library door.

Dalton nodded. "Even my mother thinks they're pretty. We have a plastic fern in our living room."

"Everywhere you go—the Laundromat, the grocery store, even the Shake Shop across the street—you see these ugly plastic plants."

Dalton laughed.

"I'm serious, Dalton Merritt. And I'm going to do something about it. I'll sneak in after school and move that plastic palm tree into a corner where nobody will see it."

"How about with the geography books? Hardly anybody looks at those."

"Good idea, Dalt. Then you'll help me?"

Dalton looked to the left and right. "Shh. This is top secret, Bert. Of course I'll help."

That afternoon Bert and Dalton waited under the staircase nearest the library until the building was completely quiet.

"Can we start now, Bert? My mother will kill me if I'm late for my piano lesson."

"What time is it?"

"Almost four."

"Okay, we'll make our move now. All we have to do is stay clear of the janitor. Wait, there he is," said Bert, shoving Dalton into a corner. The janitor passed, and they edged their way into the library.

"Almost there," said Dalton. "But how in the world are we going to carry that thing? It's bigger than both of us."

"You've got to understand how plastic plants work, Dalton. They come apart in pieces. All the better to move them."

"You're a genius, Miss Newberry," said Dalton, lifting the top off the plastic palm.

"Someday people will thank us for this."

"I DOUBT THAT VERY MUCH." It was Miss Merk, the librarian. "Roberta Newberry. Dalton Merritt. Come into my office now. And you'd better have a good explanation for this."

"Do you suppose 'for the good of humankind' will be a good enough reason?" Dalton whispered.

"Or 'in the name of good taste?'" added Bert.

"Shhh!" whispered the librarian, as she led Dalton and Bert into her office.

"Is this some sort of prank?" the librarian began.

"No, Miss Merk. We were only trying to move that ugly plastic palm," said Bert. "Everyone likes real plants."

"Of all the silly ideas. Don't you know that the school paid a good deal of money for that plant? I picked it out myself, in fact."

"But, Miss Merk, how can you stand to look at plastic plants when the real things are so much prettier?" said Bert.

"You must realize that real plants need sunlight to stay healthy and grow."

"Miss Merk, there's enough light in this room for lots of plants," Bert said. "Like snake plants, or maybe ferns."

"Are you thinking what I'm thinking, Bert?" Dalton said.

"That we could bring some of our plants and put them here in the library."

"Oh, I was thinking that I'm really late for my piano lesson, but that's a good idea too," said Dalton excitedly. He and Bert began to discuss what plants they could bring.

"One moment, please. I don't remember giving you permission." Miss Merk sighed. "Oh, all right. For one month. But you must take care of them, and if they begin to look the least bit sickly, out they go. And next time you have an idea like this, try asking first before you go moving other people's plants around."

A little more than a month later Miss Merk was giving a tour of the Cramer School Library to a visiting group of teachers. "I'm sure you'll find this plant display interesting. It's the work of some of our own students." The planter was filled with healthy Boston ferns and tall snake plants.

Bert and Dalton, studying at a nearby table, heard everything Miss Merk said. They grinned at each other.

"Well, Bert, what's our next step?"

"I'm glad you asked that, Dalt. I was eating at the Shake Shop the other day, and right next to my booth was the ugliest plastic plant . . ."

Boodge of Bonkersville

By Janette Gentry

Mr. Bangles, the bugler of Bonkersville, had a problem. In fact, it was a problem for everyone in town. The problem was Boodge. Boodge was Mr. Bangles's beagle.

Every morning Mr. Bangles said good-bye to Boodge at the front gate. He walked downtown and shinnied up the tall, tall flagpole that stood in the center of Bonkersville. Then he blew his bugle to get the children out of bed. At bedtime, he bugled softly to help them fall asleep.

Mr. Bangles had tried blowing his bugle from his balcony, his barn roof, and from the highest hill in Bonkersville. The bugle had sounded squawky and sour. From the top of the flagpole, it sounded super.

But Mr. Bangles's legs were not strong enough to climb the flagpole twice each day. So he sat in a seat on top of the flagpole doing one of his favorite things—having a picnic. All day long!

But all day long was too long for Boodge. He missed Mr. Bangles. He bayed and bayed. This set all the other dogs to baying. Bonkersville was not a peaceful place.

Mr. Bangles's neighbor, Miss Pinkel, went to see the mayor. "Something must be done," she told him. "Please call a meeting."

So the mayor called a meeting of all the grown-ups. "What can we do about Boodge?" he asked.

"There would be big, *big* trouble in Bonkersville if Mr. Bangles had to stop blowing his bugle," said one mother. "The children wouldn't sleep."

"We could stuff cotton in our ears," suggested one of the fathers.

"Good idea," said the mayor.

The next day the grownups stuffed their ears.

That didn't last long. No one could hear much of anything. And people had to shout when they talked. With all the baying and shouting, things were worse than ever.

One day Miss Pinkel didn't hear her teakettle whistle. A hole burned in the bottom. This was dangerous, and she had to buy a new teakettle.

"Please call another meeting," she shouted to the mayor.

This time one of the grandfathers had an idea. "I'll take my beagle, Barney, over to stay with Boodge," he said.

Everyone just knew the problem was solved. Barney and Boodge were friends. He would keep Boodge from being lonely.

But that didn't work either. Boodge didn't give Barney so much as a "howdy." He only bayed louder. And Barney joined right in.

The next meeting was held at night so Mr. Bangles could attend. "Boodge loves children," he told the grownups. "I think he would like to go to school with the kids."

"Boodge can be in my class," said Miss Jinkel, the art teacher.

At school, Boodge had his own desk. And he did love the children. But he kept right on baying.

Miss Jinkel was sorry to have to tell Mr. Bangles that Boodge wasn't a good pupil. "He disturbs the whole school," she said.

The mayor came to call on Mr. Bangles. "I'll bet Boodge would like to travel," the mayor said. "Would you let him join the circus?"

"Certainly not!" Mr. Bangles said.

Now the bugler was really worried. "Tomorrow I'll take you with me," he told Boodge.

Boodge was so happy that he gave Mr. Bangles a slurpy lick on the nose. But Boodge wasn't so happy when Mr. Bangles shinnied up the flagpole and left him on the ground. He gazed up at Mr. Bangles and bayed mournfully. It was time to call a meeting of the children, Mr. Bangles decided.

Little Bobby Boomerall had an idea. "It might work," said Mr. Bangles.

Early Saturday morning all Bonkersvillians gathered at the flagpole. Mr. Bangles was wearing little Bobby's red backpack. Boodge sat in the backpack. He wore a yellow baseball cap and blue sunglasses. His tail hung through a hole the children had cut in the bottom of the backpack.

Mr. Bangles had packed two big brown-bag lunches. He tied them to the backpack, one on each side. No one breathed as he started up the flagpole. Could the bugler shinny up the pole with such a load?

"I can. I can," Mr. Bangles kept telling himself as he went up . . . up . . . up. To the very top!

"No problem," Mr. Bangles yelled, as he settled himself in his seat.

The crowd cheered. "Yea, Mr. Bangles!"

When the cheering stopped, there was a great silence. Then came a soft "Ahhhhhhhhhh" from the people. How wonderful it was to hear nothing but silence!

Mr. Bangles opened one of the lunches and gave Boodge a bologna sandwich. After wolfing that down, Boodge lapped two cups of lemonade. Finally, he rested his chin on Mr. Bangles's shoulder and gave a deep sigh. He seemed to be smiling. His tail was wagging like mad!

Now Boodge sits on top of the flagpole with his beloved Mr. Bangles every day. He never bays, even when Mr. Bangles blows the bugle. All the children are as good as gold. And Bonkersville is, once again, a peaceful place.

Always A

By Linda Gillen

Archibald Ambrose Alexander Applecore had, as you can see, a very long name. But he had a very short nickname. Everybody always called him A, and his sister, Arabella Anastasia Alexandra Applecore, was always called A Also.

The Applecores, who adored animals, had an ant farm and a dog. The dog's name was Alligator. As he was a long, low, bumpy sort of dog with big teeth, the name fit him pretty well. Besides, it began with A and A Also's favorite letter of the alphabet. (You can probably guess what that was.)

All the food the Applecores ever ate began with you-know-what. They ate applesauce, apple pie, apple butter, apple cobbler, apple fritters, apple dumplings, apple pancakes, apple turnovers, and apple brown betty. They ate apricots, almonds, artichokes, American cheese, and animal crackers, also. Alligator ate all the leftovers.

Whenever the Applecores went out for a pizza, they always asked for anchovy. A and A Also didn't like anchovies at all and pushed them into little piles at the edges of their plates. They noticed little piles at the edges of their parents' plates, too. When they took the anchovies home to Alligator in a doggie bag, he nosed them into a little pile in the corner of his dish. But anchovies it always had to be. Plain pizza or pepperoni would never, never do.

One day, when A and A Also had played airplanes with Alligator all afternoon, they sat down to a supper of acorn squash, asparagus, and avocado salad, with apple cider to drink.

"Appetizing," said their father.

"Attractive," said their mother.

"Agreed," said A.

"Broccoli," said A Also.

Everyone stared at her.

"What was that?" asked Father.

"Broccoli," A Also said again, a little louder. "I want broccoli. Broccoli, *broccoli*, BROCCOLI!"

"All right, A Also," her mother said. "All right."

The next night A Also found her plate piled high with fat green stalks of broccoli. She took a bite, another bite, another, while the rest of the family watched.

Finally A had to ask. "How is it, A Also? Do you like it?"

"Well," A Also answered between chews, "it's different. It doesn't begin with an *a.*"

"But do you like it?" A asked again.

A Also chewed awhile longer. "Not so much," she announced. "But I'll like it when I grow up. And tomorrow I want celery. And doughnuts. And eggplant. And figs. Green beans. Hamburgers. Ice cream. There are lots of things I want to try that don't begin with an *a.*"

"Me, too," said A. "Me, too."

"All right, A and A Also," their mother agreed. "All right. You are amazingly adventurous, and adventurous is very good to be."

"Especially," their father added, "when you consider what letter it begins with."

"A Also," said A, "sometimes you really have good ideas."

And A Also answered, "Absolutely!"

HOLES FOR SALE

By Barbara Bartocci

Mr. Horace Holsenberry was a salesman. Not an ordinary salesman. No, indeed.

Mr. Horace Holsenberry didn't sell vacuum cleaners. Or automobiles. Or can openers. Or thumbtacks. No, indeed.

Mr. Horace Holsenberry sold holes. He sold big holes. Like swimming holes. And chimney holes.

He sold little holes. Like needle holes. And ring holes. And holes in straws and in shoes for shoelaces.

He sold good-tasting holes. Like doughnut holes.

He sold musical holes. Like flute holes. And the tiny holes in compact discs.

He sold important holes. Like keyholes.

Mr. Horace Holsenberry sold all kinds of holes.

Every morning he packed his briefcase, put on his hat, and started down the street. When he came to a house, he set down his briefcase, tugged on his tie, and knocked on the door.

"Good morning," he said cheerfully when the door opened. "My name is Holsenberry—Horace, that is—and I sell holes."

But, alas, no one seemed to care about holes. The ladies giggled and slammed the door. The men stared and looked suspicious and slammed the door.

It was very discouraging. It appeared that the bottom had dropped out of the market for holes.

But Mr. Horace Holsenberry was a very determined man. He determined to try once more. So he packed his briefcase, searched for his hat, and started down the street. When he came to a house, he set down his briefcase, tugged on his tie, and knocked on the door.

This time the door was opened by a little boy.

"Good morning. My name is Holsenberry— Horace, that is—and I sell holes."

The little boy didn't giggle or stare. He smiled.

"Hi! My name is Harold. I like holes." Harold came out and sat down on the steps. "Do you sell many holes?"

Mr. Horace Holsenberry sat down next to Harold. He sighed. "No, I don't. I have some lovely ones, too, but no one will buy them." He sighed again and put his chin in his hand. He was thinking.

Harold dangled one of his sneakers off the steps and twirled it slowly in the air. He was thinking, too. Suddenly the sneaker stopped twirling. Harold jumped up.

"I know!" he cried. "What you need to do is get rid of the holes people already have. Then they'll buy yours."

Mr. Horace Holsenberry smiled. "A splendid idea." Then he frowned. "But how do I make all the holes disappear?"

Harold's sneaker twirled some more. "I know," he said. "Magic! Do you know any magic?"

Mr. Holsenberry shook his head. But in the middle of a shake, his head stopped. He pulled a book out of his briefcase. "It seems to me I saw that word written in this book."

It was a big book. It was supposed to tell all about holes and how to sell them.

Mr. Horace Holsenberry turned the pages. Nothing on the first page. Nothing on the second.

Horace kept flipping the pages. And way in the back on the very last page, in very little letters, was the word *Magic* and some more letters.

Slowly and carefully Mr. Holsenberry looked at the letters. He looked at them for a long time.

Harold began to twitch. "What does it say?"

Mr. Horace Holsenberry shut the book, closed his eyes, and softly whispered three words. It sounded to Harold like "Horsenheffer, Happenstance, and Hoppinhoppin."

"Was that the magic?" he asked.

Mr. Holsenberry opened his eyes and smiled. "I think so," he said. "Let's go see." They walked down the sidewalk.

A big boy ran past them. He had a swimsuit in his hand and an angry frown on his face. "The swimming hole's gone!" he cried.

Mr. Horace Holsenberry smiled. So did Harold. They walked some more.

A tall, thin lady came out of her house. She held up a long, thin needle. "I can't understand it. There's no hole for my thread. How can I finish my sewing?"

A short, fat lady with a round pink box full of rings looked crossly at the tall, thin lady. "Well, I can't put on my rings," she said. "All of the holes have disappeared."

Across the street, a very busy businessman with a key in his hand was staring at his door. The key-hole was gone.

Up and down the street, in and out of houses, holes had disappeared.

Two teenage girls couldn't play their compact discs. They were quite distressed.

One young boy couldn't practice his flute. He was quite delighted.

Mothers stopped washing. The water-faucet holes were gone. Children took off their shoes. The shoelace holes were gone.

Up and down the streets, in and out of the houses, all across the village, holes had disappeared.

Mothers and fathers, boys and girls, teachers and fire fighters, even the mayor, wondered what to do. "All of the holes are gone!" the people cried. "Nothing works!"

Mr. Horace Holsenberry smiled. "I think," he said to Harold, "it's time to go see the mayor."

Mayor Moreland was walking back and forth across his office. His shoes went flap-flap because he couldn't tie the laces. His jacket went swish because the buttons had no buttonholes. Even his computer had no holes for his disks.

Mr. Horace Holsenberry knocked on the door. He was grinning ear to ear.

"Yes, yes, what is it?" said the mayor. He was quite upset and angry because he didn't know what to do.

Mr. Holsenberry tugged on his tie. "Good morning," he said cheerfully. "My name is Holsenberry —Horace, that is—and I sell holes."

The mayor stopped walking. His shoes stopped flapping. "Did you say holes?"

"Yes, indeed. I have some lovely ones, too. Would you like—"

But Mayor Moreland wasn't listening. "There's a hole salesman here!" yelled the mayor out the door. "There's a hole salesman here!" he yelled out the window.

He turned around gleefully and pulled off his shoes. "Shoelace holes!" he cried. "I'll buy eight! Buttonholes," he added. "I'll take ten."

Pretty soon Mayor Moreland's office filled up with people. Mothers and fathers, boys and girls, teachers and fire fighters, all rushed in to buy some holes.

Mr. Horace Holsenberry looked at Harold. Harold looked at him and winked. Together, they opened the briefcase. It was going to be a good day for holes after all.

FLIGHT
OF THE
ELEPHANTS

By Juanita Barrett Friedrichs

It was May again, and Miss Tuttle was planning for that most hideous, horrendous, and hazardous of all happenings—the June piano recital.

"Well, Barney," Miss Tuttle said sadly one day after his lesson, "what are you going to play at the recital?"

"Aw, come on, Miss Tuttle. Do I have to?"

"Everyone has to, Barney. Your parents have paid good money for your lessons, and they deserve to hear what you've accomplished."

When Barney started taking piano lessons at the age of six with Miss Tuttle, his parents thought he was a musical genius. By the third year, they began to have doubts. So did Barney. "Well, I don't know . . . ," he said.

Barney figured his parents did deserve some sort of punishment for making him take piano lessons, but forcing them to hear him play in a recital was going a little too far.

"You could play 'March of the Elephants'?" said Miss Tuttle, tilting her voice upward into a sad little question mark.

Barney considered. The good thing about elephants marching was that they didn't move too fast. They sort of went clomp, clomp up and down the keyboard at a nice steady pace. That gave you time to rearrange your fingers between clomps. Not enough time, but it helped.

Anyway, elephants were a lot better than monkeys. Miss Tuttle had given Barney a piece called "Monkeyshines" once, and that was a disaster. Better grab the elephants before something worse showed up.

"Okay, Miss Tuttle, but I haven't practiced that march for a long time."

"You've got four weeks. If you work hard, you can do it." Miss Tuttle sounded as sad as ever.

All through the merry month of May, Barney practiced. Outside, flowers bloomed and birds trilled. Inside, nothing but elephants. They marched all around the piano. They even marched upstairs and into Barney's mother's bedroom, where she sat with cotton in her ears.

Each week Barney took his elephants to Miss Tuttle, who grew sadder and sadder.

Finally, at their last lesson before the recital, Miss Tuttle did an astonishing thing. She smiled. *Gosh,* thought Barney, who had just seated himself at the piano, *I haven't even played a note yet.*

"Barney," said Miss Tuttle, "how well can you keep a secret?"

"Pretty well," said Barney.

Miss Tuttle winked mischievously. "Well, the other day I was looking through a stack of old cassette tapes and I found one called 'Flight of the Bumblebee.'" Barney let out a groan. "Guess what was on the other side!"

"I can't," said Barney.

"Why, 'March of the Elephants,' of course!" Miss Tuttle beamed. "I'm going to play the cassette at the recital, in the next room so no one will know. You, Barney, are going to sit at the piano and *look* as if you're playing it."

"But Miss Tuttle, I've been practicing so hard—"

"I know, dear." Miss Tuttle put a consoling arm around Barney. "But this will be much more fun. Just be sure to keep time with the music, and stop when the music stops. Now let's try it." Miss Tuttle scurried off to play the cassette.

The day of the recital, at four o'clock sharp, Barney arrived at Miss Tuttle's with his parents. Miss Tuttle approached them.

"Hello, hello," chirped Miss Tuttle gaily. "Barney, you're last on the program—the grand finale!" Miss Tuttle winked at Barney and whispered, "Just act natural, dear." Barney nodded. He glanced up at his mother to see if she had heard, but she was talking to another lady.

Finally it was Barney's turn to perform. He walked slowly to the front of the room and wiggled himself onto the piano bench, trying to act natural. Out of the corner of his eye he saw Miss Tuttle disappear into the next room.

He waited until everyone coughed, yawned, rattled their programs, creaked their chairs, and readjusted their feet. "Never begin a performance until your audience is ready," Miss Tuttle had warned.

Barney's hands were perspiring like mad. He gave them a final wipe on his trousers. From the next room Miss Tuttle waved a signal. Barney raised his hands to the keyboard and held them poised over the keys.

The audience held its breath. Barney held his breath. Everybody waited for the first clomp of "March of the Elephants."

The clomp never came. Instead, a buzzing began. It took off at one end of the keyboard and buzzed clear to the other end and back before Barney knew what was happening. "Always keep calm, no matter what goes wrong," Miss Tuttle had once said. Barney had to think fast. Miss Tuttle must have put on the wrong side of the cassette by mistake! Well, he might as well be a sport about it. Barney stopped thinking *Elephant* and forced himself to think *Bumblebee*. His hands began to fly back and forth over the keys.

But the bee was no slouch. By the time Barney's fingers got halfway up the keyboard, they met the bee on its return trip down. As if this wasn't bad enough, the stupid insect kept changing its mind. It seemed to want to fly in all directions at once.

Perspiration dripped from Barney's forehead. His arms ached. He felt dizzy. If that bee didn't buzz off soon, Barney knew *he'd* have to.

Barney sneaked a look at his audience. They were sitting wide-eyed on the edge of their seats!

39

Suddenly Barney realized he was a born performer after all. The show must go on! If he couldn't catch up to the bee with his fingers, he'd try something else. Majestically, Barney rose from the keyboard. He raised his arms and began to flap them back and forth, faster and faster. He made a buzzing noise with his tongue, louder and louder. Then he took off. Round and round the piano Barney buzzed. When the music finally stopped, he buzzed gracefully out of the room without missing a beat and landed in the waiting arms of Miss Tuttle.

The applause was thunderous. Barney just had to go back and take a bow.

How to Catch Your Very Own Elephant—
in Ten Easy Steps

By Dianne Snyder MacMurray

Before we begin, answer one question: Are you sure you really want an elephant?

Yes? Positively yes?

Read on, then. Follow the directions step by step. And I guarantee you will soon have an elephant of your very own.

1. Collect your hunting gear.

You will need:
large board
thick black crayon
hammer
nail
large mirror
stepladder
binoculars
tweezers

2. Load up your gear.

(Packing tips: Hang the mirror on your back. Hang the ladder around your neck. This way your hands and pockets are free to carry the rest.)

3. Go to the jungle and find a place where elephants like to walk.

(Hint: You should look for a spot where the grass is trampled flat.)

4. Take the large board and the crayon and make a sign that says, "Elephants Are Beautiful." Print B-I-G!

5. Nail the sign to a tree.

High up, now, so the elephants can see it.

6. Hang the mirror on a branch, right next to the sign.

7. Set up your ladder behind the mirror, climb to the top, and sit down.

This is the hardest part because there's nothing to do but wait. Don't forget, though, to keep your binoculars and tweezers handy.

If you have followed the directions closely, an elephant will come along after a while and see your sign. Of course, he'll stop to read it. (Elephants are nose-y creatures.)

ELEPHANTS ARE BEAUTIFUL

Well, now that will be a surprise! Many things have been written about elephants—elephants are huge, elephants are majestic, elephants are strong—but elephants are beautiful? Could it be true?

While he is pondering, he'll notice the mirror hanging in the tree. Of course, he'll stop to look at himself. And he'll think aloud, "If elephants are beautiful, then perhaps *I* am a beautiful elephant."

He'll spend a while in front of the mirror to see how he looks. He'll turn this way and that. First in this pose. Then in that one. There's so much to see! Now is your chance to catch him.

8. Very quietly, take out the binoculars and turn them the wrong way around.

The end you look through is the *large* end. (This is the most important part, so make sure you have it right.)

9. Point the small end of the binoculars at the elephant.

Now, what do you see? Why, the elephant shrunk to the size of a fat caterpillar.

10. Reach down with your tweezers, pick him up, and drop him (gently now!) into your shirt pocket.

There! You've got him. Your very own elephant. That's all there is to it. What you do with him now is not my concern. Of course, if your pocket is large enough, you may want to catch another to keep the first one company.

P.S. Never, never point the *big* end of the binoculars at an elephant. I once knew a hunter who did. We found his footprints, where he had run through the jungle. They were followed by the most gigantic elephant tracks anyone has ever seen.

Michael Sorts Things Out

By Susan Rote Siferd

"Michael, your bedroom is such a mess. I'm afraid that one of these days you're going to get lost in it," Mother said one night at dinner.

"If you want to go camping this weekend, Son, I think you'd better get that room cleaned up tonight after dinner," Father said.

Michael groaned and pushed away his plate of chocolate cake. He didn't even feel like eating dessert now. He trudged upstairs to his room.

He flicked on the light and picked his way around mounds of dirty clothes on the floor. He kicked aside wads of tissues and nearly fell when he slipped on some stray crayons.

He sank down onto his bed. The job was so big that he was worn out just thinking about it.

"Michael!" Mother seemed to be calling from a great distance.

The door swung open.

"Michael, are you in here?"

"Sure, Mom, I'm right over here on the bed," he answered.

"There's a bed in this room?"

Michael sat up. "Hey Mom, I can't see the doorway!" he cried. "Turn on the light."

"It *is* on, Michael."

"Mom?" He jumped up off the bed in a panic and ran right into a tower built of plastic blocks. The tower shattered, and hundreds of tiny, colored blocks flew helter-skelter.

Startled, he backed into his rocking horse, but that faithful pal only mocked him with a bobbing head and painted-on smile. Afraid to move, Michael sat down right where he was and bellowed, "I'm lost!"

"Now, don't be frightened, dear. I'm going to get help!" Mother called. Michael heard her hurry down the stairs.

Then she was running back up the stairs, and someone was shuffling heavily behind her.

"Are you sure your son didn't just run away from home?" Police Officer Meyer asked.

"It might have been easier if he had, officer," Mother answered. "At least then he would have cleared some of this junk out with him!"

Officer Meyer plunged into the room and vanished behind an overflowing bookcase.

Twenty minutes passed before he came back out with bulging pockets.

"No sign of Michael yet," he said, "but look at this!" His voice was full of wonder. "I found enough batteries in there to keep the entire police force in flashlights for a year."

Mother began to cry.

"Now, don't you cry, ma'am. I'm going right back in there to look some more. Meanwhile, why don't you call the fire department? Rescuing a kid who got lost in his own bedroom is kind of like getting a kitten down from a tree, and they do that all the time."

Still sniffling, Mother ran down the stairs. Then she was running back up the stairs, and someone was with her, singing in a rich, hearty, Irish voice that made Michael and his mother feel much better about everything.

47

"Don't be looking so worried now. Saving lives is my job!" Fire Chief O'Sullivan patted Mother on the shoulder and darted into the room.

Not five minutes had passed before he emerged, beaming like a small boy. "What did I tell you now?" he asked and reached into the front of his jacket. Out came a small ball of white fur.

"But we don't own a kitten!" Mother protested.

"Even so, I found one," Chief O'Sullivan declared, and he handed her the mewing kitten and ran back into the room.

Now Father appeared in the doorway, looking dazed and rumpled from a nap. "We've got to call in the National Guard!" he cried and ran down the stairs, two at a time.

Then there was a thunder of footsteps mounting the stairs. It sounded like an army.

It *was* an army. Company Captain Philips led his squad into Michael's room. But he leaned over too far to peer into the laundry chute and slid all the way down into the basement. One by one the other soldiers began to follow.

It occurred to Michael that he might be lost in his room forever if he waited for the grownups to find him. He stood up and looked around. It was no use. There was nothing but junk, no path going anywhere that he could see.

He glanced up at the ceiling. *From up there, I'm sure things would look different,* he thought. But how to get up there?

Then he spied his bunk bed again and scrambled up the ladder. When he turned around, everything fell into place like pieces of a puzzle.

"Hello down there!" he cried and waved to his mother and father in the doorway. Officer Meyer and Fire Chief O'Sullivan were huddled in the corner, playing an electronic video game. "What's the score?" Michael called.

"Officer Meyer's winning 7–0 . . . hey, it's Michael! We found him, everyone!" Chief O'Sullivan said, surprised.

"Company dismissed!" Captain Phillips yelled to the last of the soldiers.

The army, the Fire Chief, Officer Meyer, and especially Mother and Father all began to cheer wildly. "Our hero!" they cried. "Hurray for Michael!" they yelled.

Then the cheers died away, and there was only Mother standing in the doorway, looking amused. She tousled her son's hair.

"I thought you might like some help cleaning up this mess," she said.

"Thanks, Mom, but I think I can sort things out for myself—now," Michael answered confidently.

"But be sure to save my piece of cake from dinner. I'm going to work up an appetite. And tell Dad I'll hunt up our sleeping bags. We're going camping this weekend!"

WHAT HAPPENED TO MRS. PICKY

By Sue Santore

At first Mrs. Picky said, "I don't want any peas. I don't like food that is green." Then she said, "I won't eat carrots or sweet potatoes because they are orange." Every day Mrs. Picky refused to eat more and more different foods. She became thinner and thinner.

Mr. Picky, who did all the cooking because Mrs. Picky worked all day in a big office downtown, was upset. "You don't like my cooking! You won't eat anything any more."

"I'm sure it is very good," replied Mrs. Picky, picking at her food. "But I just can't eat things that are green, orange, brown, white, or pink."

One Saturday morning when Mrs. Picky was getting dressed, she said to Mr. Picky, "Would you look at this dress! And this and this!" None of her clothes fit. They were all too big. She put on a blue dress with a white lace collar, folded the dress over in front, and tied a scarf around her waist. "There now," she said.

Mrs. Picky grabbed her new red and gold umbrella, just in case it rained, and slipped downstairs on the banister. "I think I'll go for a long walk today. I should be back by lunchtime," she told Mr. Picky.

"All right, dear," called Mr. Picky from the kitchen. "We're having Spanish rice and cauliflower."

"Orange and white! I can't eat that," cried Mrs. Picky, as she slammed the door.

Mr. Picky sighed as he watched his wife walk briskly down the street. *She is becoming a shadow,* he thought.

I haven't had a good walk in months, thought Mrs. Picky as she strolled down the street. She looked toward Bear Mountain. There were dark clouds hovering about the top of the mountain. "It's a good thing I brought my umbrella," muttered

Mrs. Picky. She placed her large handbag on the ground and used both hands to open her umbrella. She clutched the umbrella in one hand, slipped the handbag strap over her shoulder, and off she walked.

"What a friendly breeze," said Mrs. Picky, as a small wind came up. The wind grew stronger, and the trees bent and rustled. Mrs. Picky's hair blew against her face and across her eyes. The umbrella lifted in the strong, whirling wind. Mrs. Picky held tightly to the umbrella. It lifted again and slowly carried her into the air.

"Oh, help," called Mrs. Picky. The umbrella rose higher and higher. Now she was above the tallest trees. "Oh, help! Help!" screamed Mrs. Picky, but she was so high no one heard.

As she went whirling up the side of the mountain, skimming over the treetops, Mrs. Picky gritted her teeth. She said, "I always wanted to see the top of Bear Mountain, but not this way." Mrs. Picky floated all around the mountain. Finally the wind grew weary of playing. It blew the umbrella back toward town with little, soft puffs.

High over the houses glided Mrs. Picky. "Hey there," she called, "I'm up here." But everyone was eating lunch, and no one heard her. She grabbed at the church steeple as she floated past but missed and almost lost the umbrella. There was a tall flagpole coming up. Mrs. Picky said, "Here's my chance." She grabbed the top of the flagpole with both arms and legs. Just then the wind stopped, and the umbrella fell clunking on the ground below.

Shuddering, Mrs. Picky remarked, "What if I had clunked?" She tightened her legs around the flagpole and asked herself, "What can I do now?" After thinking a moment, she plunged her hand into her purse and brought out a hammer. "I always knew this would come in handy," she said with much satisfaction. Bang! Bang! Bang! went the hammer against the flagpole. "Help! Oh please, help!" called Mrs. Picky. She shut her eyes tightly and banged loudly again.

"I will help you," said a deep voice from below.

Mrs. Picky opened her eyes and looked down. A huge gray elephant was reaching up with its long trunk. Mrs. Picky leaned toward the elephant, who lifted her gently down to the ground.

"What is an elephant doing in the middle of town?" asked Mrs. Picky.

"My zoo keeper forgot to lock my cage door, and I decided to take a walk," replied the elephant. "My name is Junie Jumbo. What were you doing on a flagpole in the middle of town?"

Mrs. Picky blushed. "The wind blew me. Thank you very much for helping me down."

"Don't mention it," replied Junie Jumbo, "but, if you are tired of this umbrella you threw down, may I have it?"

Mrs. Picky looked away from the umbrella and shuddered. "Of course," she said. "Good-bye, and thanks again."

"See you at the zoo sometime," Junie said and lumbered off.

At the zoo Jack Jumbo said to his wife, "The keeper was looking all over for you. Where have you been, dear, and where did you get that red and gold umbrella?"

"You would never believe it," Junie Jumbo replied between bites of hay.

Mrs. Picky scurried home. She quickly washed for lunch and hastened into the kitchen.

"You are late, dear. What happened?" asked Mr. Picky, as he stirred the Spanish rice.

"You would never believe it," Mrs. Picky replied. And she ate everything on her plate.

RUTABAGA SUMMER

By William Ashworth

"Rutabaga?" asked Danny Morgan.

His friend Ron Franklin smiled. "Rutabaga," he said. "It's a vegetable of some kind."

"What do rutabagas look like?"

"Something like a turnip. I heard my mom and dad talking about them last night."

"What do they taste like?"

"Don't know," said Ron. He shrugged his shoulders. "All I know is, it's an awfully funny name. Rutabaga."

"Rutabaga," said Danny. And they both burst out laughing, rolling over and over in the green June grass. They were five days out of third grade. Fourth grade was a long time off. The sky was blue, the air was cool and fresh, and there were rutabagas in the world.

Danny leaped to his feet. "Race you to my house!" he called out. "Last one there is a rutabaga!" It was the beginning of what would later be called the Rutabaga Summer.

Breathless and laughing, Danny and Ron tumbled into the kitchen where Danny's mother was making cookies. "Mom," asked Danny, "have I ever tasted a rutabaga?"

"No," said his mother. "I don't think so, anyway." She pointed to a pan of cookies cooling beside the stove. "Have a cookie," she said.

"Are they rutabaga cookies?" asked Ron.

"Goodness, no!" said Danny's mother. "At least I hope not!"

"Well, I'm going to pretend they are," said Danny, taking one. "Rutabaga cookies." And he giggled. "Rutabaga, rutabaga."

And that was the pattern of the way things would be during Rutabaga Summer.

When they played games, someone was always Mr. Rutabaga. When they played cars, they got gas at the Rutabaga Garage. When they got mad at things, they yelled, "Oh, rutabaga!" Ron's yellow slot-car racer was rutabaga-colored. The boxcars on Danny's electric train delivered rutabagas. They organized a pretend insurance company called Morgan, Franklin, and Rutabaga.

They started a neighborhood newspaper, *The Herald-Rutabaga*.

They told rutabaga riddles: What's round and yellow and goes buzz, buzz, buzz? An electric rutabaga.

In June, they ran a lemonade stand that advertised RUTABAGA JUICE.

In July, they asked the man who came around on the ice-cream truck if he had any rutabaga ice cream. He said he didn't think so.

In August, Danny called his sister "Rutabaga-face," and she cried, and his mother scolded him and went out to talk to Ron's mother over the back fence.

"Are you, by any chance," she asked, "getting tired of rutabagas?"

"I am indeed," said Ron's mother.

"Do you have any ideas about how to stop the rutabagas?"

"I am working on one," said Ron's mother. "As of yet, it's only an idea."

"I wish you luck," said Danny's mother, and she went back into the house.

The next day, Danny came to his mother and asked if he could sleep out in Ron's back yard that night. "He invited me," he said. "And his mother said it was all right."

"If his mother said it was all right, then it's all right," said Danny's mother. So Danny took his sleeping bag and his cowboy hat and his checkers and went over to Ron's. They had a great time all afternoon. First they played Monopoly. ("Go directly to jail, do not pass go, do not collect 200 rutabagas.") Then they played Mad Scientist. ("I warn you, I am inventing a way to turn you into a rutabaga!") Then they went outside and played cowboys and rutabagas. Then they played . . .

"Suppertime," said Ron's mother.

The main dish for supper was stew. Ron and Danny each heaped great portions on their plates. After a couple of bites Ron stopped eating.

"Hey," said Ron, "what tastes weird?"

"What looks weird?" asked Danny. He held up something on the end of his fork. It was a funny yellow color and looked a little bit like a potato, but it didn't taste at all like a potato.

"Do you boys know what that is?" asked Ron's mother suspiciously.

Danny and Ron looked at it. They looked at each other. They looked at Ron's mother. "It's a rutabaga!" exploded Ron.

"That's exactly right," said his mother. "How does it taste?"

"Eeeuuuchchchch!!!" said Danny and Ron together.

Later that evening, just before it was time for the boys to go to bed, Ron's father wandered out to the kitchen, where his wife was getting a snack of fruit for all of them. "Madge, you're an absolute genius," he said. "I haven't heard a 'rutabaga' all evening."

"I know," smiled Ron's mother. "Isn't it wonderful?" She topped each bowl with a round yellow fruit. "Ron! Danny!" she called. "Time for your snack and then bed."

Ron and Danny rushed into the kitchen. They looked at the bowls of fruit.

"Hey, what's that funny-looking yellow one on top?" asked Ron.

"That's a kumquat," said his mother.

"Kumquat," said Ron. He looked at Danny.

Danny looked back. He chuckled. Then he giggled. "Kumquat," he said.

"Kumquat!" they yelled together.

The smiles on the faces of Ron's parents faded.

"Let's go put on our pajamas," said Danny. He took off at top speed, calling back over his shoulder, "Last one to the bathroom is a kumquat!"

And so the Rutabaga Summer ended.

And Kumquat Fall began!

The Christmas Goose

By Terri Dennison

My sister Becca has the silliest ideas. One of her silliest was when she wanted to get Mom and Dad something really special for Christmas. Becca overheard Grandma remembering how they always had a goose when she was young. Becca snapped her fingers.

"That's it," she told me. "Eric, could you help me find a goose?"

"Try the supermarket, poultry section."

Becca frowned. "I mean a live goose."

"A Christmas goose is always cooked. That's what Grandma meant."

"No." Becca shook her head. "Look at the pictures on the wrapping paper and cards. There's always a beautiful goose with a red ribbon around its neck. So walk with me to the pet store. Okay?"

I put on my coat. It was never any use arguing with her.

"A goose?" The salesclerk looked over Becca's head at me. I just shrugged. It wasn't my idea. "You might try a farm," he suggested.

"Forget it," I told Becca. "I don't know any farmers, and you don't either."

"If I find a goose, will you help me get it home?"

"Sure," I agreed readily. There was no way she would find a goose.

I was wrong. Becca cornered me after school the next day. "My friend's cousin has a goose," she said. "She got it in her Easter basket, but she doesn't want it anymore."

That sounded suspicious. "Why not?" I asked.

Becca shrugged. "Who cares? I've got her address, and you promised you would help me get it home."

We took the bus across town. Becca's friend's cousin showed us the goose. I never realized how big geese are, until this one came at me, white wings raised. Right from the start, that goose hated me. But Becca loved it.

"How are we going to get it home?" I asked.

"It always follows me when I give it corn," the cousin said.

"What if it gets full? At the rate Becca is feeding it, it can't eat much more."

"My dad once carried it in a grocery sack."

That sounded good to me. I reached out to grab the goose. It dodged. I dove for it. The goose squawked, then hissing, came straight at me. I ran. The goose chased me around the yard, clacking its beak and flapping its wings.

"Get it away from me," I yelled, scrambling up an apple tree. Becca lured it away with corn. I waited until it was clear across the yard before coming down. Geese have hard beaks.

We slipped a sack over its head while it was eating. Once in the dark, the goose let me carry it. Becca carried the sack of corn.

The driver looked at us suspiciously as we got on the bus. "What have you kids got?" he asked.

"A goose," I said.

He stared at me a minute, then smiled and waved us on back.

We settled into our seats, and I tried to ignore the twenty-pound goose squishing my arm.

"Eric," Becca whispered, "is the goose all right? You don't think it will suffocate in there, do you?"

"It's okay. I'm sure."

"I'm just going to take a peek." Before I could stop her, Becca opened a corner of the sack. As soon as the goose saw the light, it went wild. The woman next to us shrieked. The goose honked. The bus screeched to a stop.

"Don't hurt him," Becca yelled. "Catch it, Eric."

I tried, but that goose really hates me. The driver chased the goose to the back of the bus. It slipped between his legs and half ran, half flew forward again. I lunged for it but missed. Feathers flew all over the place.

"Get the corn," I yelled to Becca.

She scattered some corn. The goose finally calmed down to eat. We put the sack over its head, and I took a firm hold. It wasn't going to get away again.

The driver was furious as he put us off the bus. How could I have known he thought the goose was frozen? At this point, I wished that it was.

"What now?" I asked Becca. "I can't lug this thing all the way home."

"Maybe it will walk part of the way by itself."

"No way. We're not opening this bag again until we're safe at home." So I carried it all the way.

I let the goose go in the back yard, then went inside to flop on the couch. My arms ached.

"Eric." Becca looked worried. "Where can we hide it?"

"Not my problem," I muttered, switching on the TV. I just wanted to forget about that goose.

Becca hid it in my treehouse. I was too tired to argue with her.

On Christmas morning Becca led us into the kitchen. There was the goose, calmly eating corn. It never stopped eating. Becca had put a big red ribbon around its neck.

"Oh, Becca," Mom said, then stopped.

"It's a goose," I explained.

"A Christmas goose, just like Grandma's," Becca said. She looked at me. "It's from both of us," she added, smiling.

"It certainly is . . . uh . . . special," Dad said.

Becca grinned from ear to ear. I grinned, too. I guess she was right. That goose did look pretty special. I just hope that next year she thinks of something easier for us to give Mom and Dad— like a garden rake or a mixing bowl. But then she wouldn't be Becca, would she?

The String Collection

By Mary Radloff

Mr. Fergus was a collector. He collected bottles with pretty shapes, boxes of all sizes, rocks of many colors, and seashells from the beaches of the world.

One day as Mr. Fergus was walking down Main Street in the town of Sunnyvale, he found a piece of string. It was short, sturdy, and a lovely shade of red. Mr. Fergus stooped down and picked it up. He looked at the string.

"This," said Mr. Fergus to himself, "is the beginning of my string collection!"

He wound the piece of red string into a ball and put it in his pocket. Mr. Fergus stopped at the meat market for a pound of hamburger for supper. He was pleased to see the butcher tie the package with a piece of white string.

When Mr. Fergus got home, he removed the white string from the package, tied one end to the end of his ball of red string, and wound it around. The ball of string was now a little larger.

Mr. Fergus put the ball in a special drawer and marked it with the words "String Collection."

Every day Mr. Fergus added to his string collection. He bought new shoes, and the clerk tied the box with soft brown string. Mr. Fergus tied the brown string to the end of his collection and wound it around. The ball grew larger.

He bought three shirts at the big department store and carried them home by the strong green string around the package. He tied the end of the green string to his collection and wound it around. The ball grew larger.

Several times the newspaper carrier ran out of rubber bands and tied Mr. Fergus's paper with blue string instead. Mr. Fergus tied the blue string to his collection. The ball grew larger.

One day the letter carrier delivered a book. The package was tied with fuzzy black string. Mr. Fergus tied the black string to his collection and wound it around. The ball grew larger.

Soon Mr. Fergus's string collection was so large it would no longer fit in the drawer. He moved it to a shelf in the kitchen. One night the huge ball rolled right off the shelf. It made a loud thumping noise, and Mr. Fergus had to get out of bed to see what was the matter. After that, he just left the collection on the floor.

When spring came, Mr. Fergus barely managed to roll the large ball of string through the kitchen door and out into the back yard. It looked bright and cheerful there with the grass showing green around it and a few tulips adding a red color of their own along the fence.

Soon the children of Sunnyvale learned of Mr. Fergus's string collection. They began to bring him string from lunch bags, string from old pull toys, and string they found in drawers at home.

The string collection grew so large that Mr. Fergus had to use his ladder to reach the top of the ball to tie and wind more string. He was so busy tying and winding he had no time at all for collecting bottles, boxes, rocks, or shells from the beaches of the world.

Now the ball of string was so large it filled his entire back yard. He had no room for flowers, no room for grass.

The ball of string was so large that it shaded his entire kitchen window, making the room very dark and gloomy.

"This is enough!" cried Mr. Fergus at the end of one long day spent in tying and winding string.

"I am through collecting string. I am through tying and winding. I want my yard back with green grass and flowers. I am no longer a collector of strings!"

Mr. Fergus felt much better after that, but he still had one problem. He still had a yard full of a ball of string. It was too big to carry; it was too heavy to lift; it was too large to roll. How would he ever get rid of such a large collection of string?

Mr. Fergus thought and thought. At last a slow smile spread over his face. Mr. Fergus had a good idea! He went into his house and was very busy with paper, sticks, rags, and even a bit of string. He hummed as he worked and a few times he chuckled. He went to bed that night a happy man.

The next day was bright and sunny. Mr. Fergus did nothing.

The second day was cool and rainy. Mr. Fergus did nothing.

The third day was brisk and windy. Mr. Fergus went out carrying the paper-stick-rag-string-thing he had made. He tied one end of it to the end of his string collection. It looked a little like—very much like it—like it was a kite!

Mr. Fergus waited for a good gust of wind and tossed the kite into the air. It whirled and swirled. It dipped and slipped. As the kite went up, it took with it Mr. Fergus's string collection. As the kite went higher, the ball of string grew smaller. All the children of Sunnyvale came to watch. All morning, all afternoon, on into the early evening the ball of string disappeared as the kite disappeared. At last both the kite and the collection were gone forever.

"Hurrah!" cheered the children.

Just then the wind tossed a little feather at the feet of Mr. Fergus.

"Hmm," said Mr. Fergus, as he stooped to pick it up. "This is the start of my new collection!"

The Wizard's Apprentice

By D.L. Halterman

"You must be very careful in my workshop. This whole room is charged with magical powers." The Wizard peered at his young apprentice over the small round glasses that were perched on the tip of his nose.

When the Wizard spoke, small blue sparks flittered about his tall cone-shaped hat covered with bright silver stars. A slight odor of something burning tickled Amanda's nose.

"Oh, yes, I will," Amanda almost whispered. She tingled with excitement at the thought of her first day of working with the Wizard.

"In fact," the Wizard continued, pulling thoughtfully on his long white beard, "not so long ago . . ."

"Excuse me," Amanda interrupted by putting a finger under her nose.

"I think I'm going to . . . ACHOO!" She sneezed.

"I was right in the middle of a great spell . . . ." the Wizard began again.

Amanda giggled.

"Young lady, I can't teach you anything if you keep interrupting me," the Wizard said gruffly.

"But there's a frog on your head." Amanda was trying not to laugh.

A small green frog peered out from under the Wizard's hat.

"Oh, no. I hope that sneeze didn't start it again," the Wizard moaned. He removed the frog from his head, held it in one hand, and snapped his fingers. It disappeared.

"Start what?" Amanda asked, then squealed with surprise when several more frogs of various colors suddenly appeared about the room. A bright red one sat upon the Wizard's shoulder.

"FROGS!" the Wizard shouted. "Lots of FROGS . . . Don't move, don't do anything," he warned her.

Amanda tried not to, but the tip of her nose itched so badly she couldn't stand it. She had to scratch it.

The instant she did, more frogs magically appeared all about the room. Bright yellow ones covered the Wizard's desk; red ones and blue ones were appearing so fast there was barely enough room on the floor for a decent hop.

"Oh, dear, now look what you've done," the Wizard cried. He started to clap his hands together to stop the frogs from coming, but one suddenly appeared in each of his hands.

Thinking she could help, Amanda clapped *her* hands together.

"No, don't do that!" the Wizard yelled.

It was too late. The Wizard vanished!

Amanda looked around the room. Frogs were everywhere, and more were coming every second.

A large bright orange one sat between her feet. It had a tiny cone-shaped hat on its head.

It was the Wizard!

"Oh, no! I didn't mean to turn you into a frog," Amanda cried. She gently picked him up and held him before her.

The Wizard blinked his large bulging eyes and stuck his tongue out at Amanda. He did not look like a happy frog.

"I'm sorry," she said, "but you don't have to get nasty about it!"

He hopped up and down in her hands and pointed at his desk.

"Your Magical book!" Amanda exclaimed. She carefully picked her way through the frogs on the floor and plopped the Wizard on his desk.

"Frogs, frogs, frogs," she mumbled brushing frogs off the ancient book with strange symbols marked in gold on its cracked and worn cover.

With the Wizard looking on she quickly turned the yellowed pages. Suddenly the Wizard hopped onto one of the pages and made small excited croaking sounds.

Quickly reading the directions on the page, Amanda carefully balanced on her right foot and clapped her hands three times.

She was relieved when all the red frogs disappeared without a trace.

Four claps and the yellow frogs were gone.

Five and the blue frogs vanished.

"Oh, great! I forgot the green ones," she moaned.

Again she raised her hands before her and clapped twice . . . . Nothing happened.

Twice more and the green frogs turned into black bats that screamed around the room diving at the poor Wizard.

"I forgot to stand on my right foot," Amanda said angrily.

She stomped her foot on the floor and slammed the Magical book shut just as the Wizard hopped between the pages to hide from the bats.

Instantly it was very quiet in the room. So quiet Amanda could hear her own heartbeat. All the frogs and bats were gone.

"Well, now I've done it!" Amanda sighed. Carefully she opened the Magical book and peeked in. The Wizard was gone!

"Actually, you did rather well," said the Wizard.

Amanda looked around the room . . . then . . . up.

"Are you all right?" she asked.

"Quite all right," said the Wizard sitting on a large wooden beam near the ceiling, "and I think you have learned a valuable lesson," he smiled.

"Right," agreed Amanda. "Never do this!" she said clapping her hands together.

"Ribbit!" said a large purple frog that suddenly appeared in front of Amanda.

"Oh, oh, not again," she said.

"I think I'll just stay up here this time!" the Wizard laughed.

Donkey at Madison and Hanna

By Marie P. Knott

It was nearly midnight as Deputy Fred Sherman drove his patrol car away from headquarters. "Just once," he mused, "just once, I'd like a night without having to chase a reckless driver or ticket some speeder. My job would be easy if all drivers understood the importance of obeying speed limits," he thought out loud, as he cruised along.

"Calling Car 29," the dispatcher's voice interrupted. "Proceed to intersection of Madison and Hanna. A donkey reported to be obstructing traffic."

A donkey at midnight! *Probably a joke,* Deputy Sherman thought, as he headed his car toward the intersection.

But it wasn't a joke. When he reached the corner, his headlights shone straight into the eyes of a real donkey. The deputy parked the car, leaving the flashing red light on. Then he walked over to the donkey.

"Come on, fella, get out of the way!" he ordered.

The donkey stood still.

The deputy tugged; he pushed; he coaxed. The animal refused to budge.

Finally the deputy returned to his car and radioed headquarters for help. Then he walked back to the donkey.

"Come on, fella, you'd better move," he urged. "You don't want to get hit by a car, do you?"

But "fella" didn't seem to care. The deputy tried pushing again. Then he climbed on the donkey's back. The donkey looked around as if to say, "Oh, would you like a ride?" And off he walked.

The deputy rode around and around as the donkey chose the path. "At least we're moving now," the deputy said to himself. But what could he do with the animal?

Cars drove by without disturbing the donkey. A tow truck from Stone's Garage approached. The animal halted. The deputy dismounted. "You stay here," he said to the donkey.

Alex Stone got out of the truck. "Headquarters called me," he said. "Maybe I can tow him to the garage." He looked at the donkey. "What, no bridle? Nothing to hitch to? I can't tow him this way."

"Well, maybe he can ride up front," the deputy offered sheepishly. Meanwhile, the donkey wandered back into the road.

"Come on, fella," the deputy coaxed again. "I know you can move."

But "fella" didn't move. The deputy tugged and Alex pushed. Then Alex tugged while the deputy pushed. The results were the same. None!

Alex laughed. "Well, you can't give him a ticket for speeding," he said.

At this moment a pickup truck stopped. Its front bumper had pushed many stalled cars. Its driver, Henry Stone, hopped out to survey the situation.

"A little push should take care of this problem," he decided.

Henry eased the truck up to the donkey and gently pushed. But the animal planted his feet firmly. A truck was not going to push him very far. Henry stopped the truck.

Alex laughed. He called, "Henry, he doesn't play your game, either."

The three men gathered together to discuss their problem. "Let's call my brother Bill," suggested Henry. "Maybe he will have an idea."

Bill Stone was awakened by the ringing of his phone. "Bill, we need help. Alex and I were called by Deputy Sherman to move a donkey off the road at Madison and Hanna."

Soon Bill arrived in another truck. He heard the story of the obstinate donkey.

"We can't push him or tow him. He just won't move," ended Alex.

"Deputy, you say he moved with you on his back. Suppose you ride him again. The rest of us will try to maneuver him onto the truck. Then I can haul him to the garage." Bill looked at the donkey. "And let's have a little cooperation from you this time!"

The scheme worked at first. The deputy got on the donkey's back. Bill started the motor. But that was cooperation enough, it seemed. The donkey kicked, and the deputy landed on the ground.

"Why don't you go back where you belong?" inquired the deputy.

But the donkey was not inclined to go where he belonged. He didn't intend to move or to be moved unless he wanted to. He walked up to the side of the truck.

Bill reached out and rubbed the donkey's ear. "Why don't you move, old boy? I'd like to finish my sleep." Bill continued talking as he cautiously put the engine in gear. The truck moved. To the amazement of the men, the donkey moved, too.

Bill drove, one hand on the steering wheel, the other rubbing the donkey's ear. The other men followed in their cars.

The procession finally reached the center of town. Here the donkey stopped. Again, no amount of pushing, tugging, coaxing, or ear-rubbing would induce him to move.

Alex broke a long silence. "Maybe he's a Mexican burro and only understands Spanish."

"Big help that is—unless you speak Spanish, or Burro," grunted the deputy.

"I don't, but Joe Borillo does," replied Alex.

"Joe Borillo speaks Burro?" asked Bill.

"No, Spanish. He lives across the street," replied Alex. "I'll go get him."

Soon Joe arrived and spoke in Spanish to the donkey, but he didn't seem to understand Spanish, either.

The deputy decided to try riding him again. The donkey looked around as if to say, "Oh, it's you again!" Off he walked with the deputy on his back. The deputy breathed a sigh of relief.

Alex, Henry, and Bill followed in their trucks. Together they managed to steer the donkey into Stone's Garage. They tied him up securely and shut the garage door.

"Car 29 calling dispatcher."

"Go ahead."

"The donkey is no longer obstructing traffic. He is tied up in Stone's Garage."

It was now seven o'clock in the morning. Deputy Sherman completed his patrol and reported to headquarters at eight o'clock.

"You must have had a quiet night," said the chief as he looked over the report. "No accidents. No reckless drivers. No speeders. That's the kind of night every police officer dreams about."

But to the deputy it had been a nightmare. And all due to just one little donkey!

Noodletoo

By B.L. Dickinson

I was bored. There was nothing to do. Mom gave me a long piece of red yarn and some large macaroni noodles. I decided to make a noodle necklace with them. Mom said she would help me put the yarn through the noodles if I had trouble with it. I thought I could do it.

I wonder if there are noodles everywhere. I wonder if there are noodles on the moon. I asked my mom when she came to tie a knot in the yarn. She put the necklace over my head and said she didn't think there were noodles in space. I told her I'm going to pretend there are. She told me to use my noodle and have a good time.

I'll pretend I'm going on an adventure to another planet! But which planet? Not Pluto. It's too cold there. Not Venus. Way too hot. I'll take a trip to NOODLETOO! A make-believe trip can be to a make-believe place.

I'll put on my astronaut suit. Zip it up. Now my space boots. Lace them up. Last of all, my helmet. There, I'm ready for takeoff!

I crawl under the table and into my spaceship. Ten, nine, eight, seven, six, five, four, three, two, one, blast-off! NOODLETOO, here I come!

I can see a steamy planet through my spaceship window. It must be NOODLETOO because when we cook noodles, they make steam.

I'm coming in for a landing! Ten, nine, eight, seven, six, five, four, three, two, one, splooshdown!

I'm stepping out of my rocket and putting my feet in . . . noodles! Soft, steamy pasta. I can see spaghetti, lasagna, fettucini, all kinds of pasta, everywhere! I sniff the warm breeze. It smells like cheese and tomato sauce. Yummy!

I wonder if anyone lives on this planet. Wait . . . what's this? I see a box on a large, flat lasagna noodle. I walk and bounce over to it. It looks like a lunch box. There is a name on it—Mac A. Roni. Someone named Mac must live here.

I hear noises! I hear voices! My heart is beating on my ribs! I'm afraid. What if the voices are coming from monsters! Space monsters! NOODLETOO monsters! I hide behind a large pasta shell. The voices are louder. They don't sound like monster voices. They sound like children . . . happy children.

I move to the other side of the shell and peek around the edge. Oh, my! I see little pasta people playing in a pasta playground. They are swinging on strings of linguini and sliding down huge pieces of ruffled lasagna.

I hear someone call, "Resauce is over. Time to come inside." The little pasta people are running at me! Wait . . . no . . . they are not after me. They are disappearing into their pasta shell!

I put my ear against the pasta wall. I can hear someone say, "Take out your pencils and paper, class." This must be a school. I lean around the corner of the shell. I can see a sort of doorway. There is a sign hanging by pieces of spaghetti. The sign says Elbow Room.

I move behind the pasta. I know it's okay to be different, but this place is super strange! I guess these pasta people would think Earth is strange, too.

"Hey, Mac!"

What's that? Someone's coming! I jump and slide into a huge manicotti tunnel.

"Wait up, Mac! You forgot your lunch box."

Two little pasta people walk past me. Whew, they didn't notice me hiding in here!

"Thanks. My mom would have been upset with me if I forgot it again."

"Yeah. I know what you mean. Is there meatball practice today?"

"The coach said there would be practice if it doesn't sprinkle."

"Aw, a little Parmesan never hurt anyone. I hope we don't have to cancel."

"Me too. I have to get home. See you."

" 'Bye."

That's really weird! Meatball practice? Parmesan rain? I think I'd better get back to Earth.

I crawl out of the big noodle and sneak back to my spaceship. Ten, nine, eight, seven, six, five, four, three, two, one, blast-off! Good-bye, NOODLETOO . . . Hello, Earth!

My spaceship lands safely under the table. It's good to be home. Mom says, "Welcome back. Go wash up for dinner. We're having your favorite— spaghetti."

I wonder if pasta people ever take pretend trips to Earth. I hope so.

The Fabulous Royal Junque

By Carolyn Kane

Once there was a King who loved junk. Every closet in his royal palace was filled with old crowns and musty royal robes that had been out of style for a hundred years. Whenever the King opened a closet, a tarnished crown would fall from the top shelf and hit him on the head.

The tower room was stuffed with rusty swords and tattered capes. The cabinets of the palace kitchen were crammed with broken cauldrons and cracked goblets. But the biggest junk-heap of all was in the royal basement, which was filled with thousands of worn-out things. There were magic rings that had lost their magic, seven-league boots that were too old to travel any farther than the next block, invisible cloaks that were full of moth holes, and flying carpets that floated helplessly in mid-air. There were also faded jewels, tattered books, old letters, buttons, buckles, fans, and bottles covered with goo.

The King loved his junk so much that he could never throw anything away. Together with his favorite nephew, Prince Peterkin of Pergola, he spent many happy hours in the basement, sifting through his old things and admiring them.

"Look, Peterkin!" he would say. "A book of genuine magic spells."

"Do you suppose any of them still work?" Peterkin would ask.

"You could never find any of the ingredients in a modern drug store. But look at this!—a real magic wand!"

"It's pretty rusty, isn't it? Does it still work?"

"Oh, heavens, the magic in this wand must have worn off before my great-grandfather was crowned king. But if we polished it with unicorn oil, it would glisten like a thousand diamonds."

"Where will we get unicorn oil?"

"Maybe we'll find some old unicorn oil in these gooey bottles."

As the years went by, the King's collection of junk became too large for the closets, the tower room, or even the basement. Swords, capes, rings, and wands began to pile up in the guest bedrooms, in the ballroom, and even in the royal throne room, until there was no place for the King to entertain his visitors. When the Mayor came to tea, he had to sit on the terrace even if a thunderstorm was raging, because there was no longer any place to serve tea indoors.

One day the Mayor grew angry. "Enough is enough, Your Majesty!" he shouted. "I've swallowed half a hurricane with my tea! You can't rule this kingdom properly if you force all of your most important subjects to sit outside in the rain whenever they come to visit you."

"But what can I do?" said the King sadly. "You know how I am—I just can't bear to throw anything away. It's too painful."

"I'll call Pitchit and Sons Trash Removal Service," said the Mayor. "They're the best trash removers in the whole kingdom! They'll load all of your worthless old things onto a giant garbage truck and heave them into the city dump! At last you'll be rid of your trash and have a clean palace again."

"Trash!" shouted the King. "Mr. Mayor, how dare you refer to my beautiful junk as *trash!*" But in his heart he knew that the Mayor was right. So the next day Mr. Pitchit came in his white uniform, and he brought his seven sons. They gathered up every sword, every buckle, every worn-out magic wand—even the bottles covered with goo—and piled them onto their truck in a rusty, dusty, tarnished heap. The King was too sad to watch the Pitchits take his things away. He sat on the terrace, sipping weak tea from a cracked cup and trying not to look at the Pitchit truck.

Prince Peterkin of Pergola was sad, too. Even though he had never loved junk as much as the King did, he would miss exploring the basement with his uncle. "Maybe a walk would cheer me up," said Peterkin. So he walked to town, but his shoulders slumped and his feet dragged.

"I was getting to like all that junk," said Peterkin to himself. "Going to visit the King was always like going to a museum. If only—"

Suddenly Peterkin had an idea. "That's it!—I know how to save my uncle's Royal Junk!" he cried. His shoulders straightened, and he started to run to the auction house.

An hour later, just as the Pitchit's dump truck was starting to pull away from the palace, Peterkin came running into the courtyard. With him was a tall woman in a blue suit.

"Stop!" she shouted. "I'm Dr. Silvertone, the royal auctioneer. Where are you going with that cargo of priceless treasures and beautiful antiques?"

"Cargo?" said Mr. Pitchit. "This is a load of garbage. Look, these bottles are covered with goo."

"That's not goo!" said Dr. Silvertone. "That's some of the original lava from Mount Vesuvius, the famous volcano."

"But everything is covered with dust—see?" said Mr. Pitchit. He puckered his lips to blow some of the dust away.

Dr. Silvertone looked as if she would faint. "*Stop!*—that's the original dust that gathered on King Arthur's sword before he pulled it out of the stone. It's priceless!

"Remember," she added solemnly, "today's trash is sometimes tomorrow's treasure."

The King, who had come down from the terrace to see what was going on, was beaming happily at Dr. Silvertone. "I like your attitude," he said. "Tell these men to put all of my treasures back where they were."

"No!—they're much too fragile to move," she said. "Your Majesty, you'll have to build a museum around them."

"Yes!" said Prince Peterkin, leaping for joy. "The National Museum of Fabulous Royal Junk!"

"Let's make that 'Junque' with a 'Q-U-E,'" said Dr. Silvertone. "It's more clever and grand."

So the King had both a clean palace and a beautiful museum where he could visit his royal junque every day. People came from miles around to see the dust from King Arthur's sword. The King liked Dr. Silvertone so much that he married her and made her his Queen, and the two of them spent every weekend traveling to garage sales to find new junque for their museum.